The Best of Poe

Edgar Allan Poe

ILLUSTRATED

Pendulum Press, Inc.

West Haven, Connecticut

ISBN 0-88301-093-3 Complete Set
        0-88301-269-3 This Volume

Library of Congress Catalog Card Number 77-79443

Published by
Pendulum Press, Inc.
An Academic Industries, Inc. Company
The Academic Building
Saw Mill Road
West Haven, Connecticut 06516

Printed in the United States of America

to the teacher

Pendulum Press is proud to offer the NOW AGE ILLUSTRATED Series to schools throughout the country. This completely new series has been prepared by the finest artists and illustrators from around the world. The script adaptations have been prepared by professional writers and revised by qualified reading consultants.

Implicit in the development of the Series are several assumptions. Within the limits of propriety, anything a child reads and/or wants to read is *per se* an educational tool. Educators have long recognized this and have clamored for materials that incorporate this premise. The sustained popularity of the illustrated format, for example, has been documented, but it has not been fully utilized for educational purposes. Out of this realization, the NOW AGE ILLUSTRATED Series evolved.

In the actual reading process, the illustrated panel encourages and supports the student's desire to read printed words. The combination of words and picture helps the student to a greater understanding of the subject; and understanding, that comes from reading, creates the desire for more reading.

The final assumption is that reading as an end in itself is self-defeating. Children are motivated to read material that satisfies their quest for knowledge and understanding of their world. In this Series, they are exposed to some of the greatest stories, authors, and characters in the English language. The Series will stimulate their desire to read the original edition when their reading skills are sufficiently developed. More importantly, reading books in the NOW AGE ILLUS-TRATED Series will help students establish a mental "pegboard" of information — images, names, and concepts — to which they are exposed. Let's assume, for example, that a child sees a television commercial which features Huck Finn in some way. If he has read the NOW AGE Huck Finn, the TV reference has meaning for him which gives the child a surge of satisfaction and accomplishment.

After using the NOW AGE ILLUSTRATED editions, we know that you will share our enthusiasm about the Series and its concept.

—The Editors

about the author

Edgar Allan Poe was born in 1809 in Boston, Massachusetts. Left an orphan at the age of two, he was adopted in 1811 by his uncle, John Allan of Richmond, Virginia. He entered the University of Virginia, but left because he was always drinking and gambling rather than studying. He was later dismissed from West Point for repeatedly breaking the rules. When John Allan died in 1834, Poe was left penniless and rejected.

In 1836 Poe married his thirteen-year-old cousin, Virginia Clemm. Their life was hard, since Poe made very little money from his writing. When Virginia died in 1847, Poe began to drink and gamble more than ever, causing him to live in constant misery. His short stories, however, were becoming popular—even in Europe, where they were translated into French by such writers as Baudelaire and Mallarmé.

Throughout his career, Poe suffered long periods of sickness bordering on insanity. This and his continual drinking made him often fear that he was losing his mind entirely. The end came in 1849 when he was found dying in a Baltimore gutter. Edgar Allan Poe was one of the most misunderstood men of his time—but he was also one of America's greatest short story writers.

Edgar Allan Poe

The Best Of
POE

Adapted by
NAUNERLE FARR

Illustrated by
G. TALOAC
N. REDONDO
N. ZAMORA
E. R. CRUZ

a
VINCENT FAGO
production

The Pit and the Pendulum

In a dream—a nightmare—
I saw the lips of the black-
robed judges as they
sentenced me to death.
But first I would go to
prison. I fainted from
fear.

There were shadow memories of tall figures that lifted and carried me down . . .

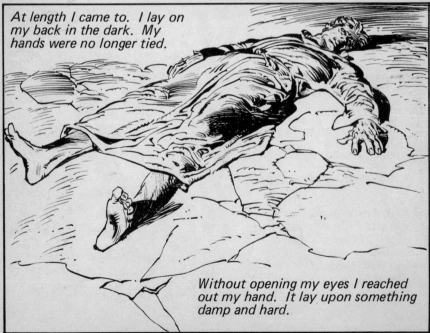

At length I came to. I lay on my back in the dark. My hands were no longer tied.

Without opening my eyes I reached out my hand. It lay upon something damp and hard.

I was afraid to open my eyes, afraid that I would see—nothing! I tried, and it was so! There was only the dark.

I leaped to my feet and reached wildly in all directions. I was afraid I would feel the walls of a tomb!*

At length my hands found a wall, smooth, slimy, and cold. I walked around it trying to figure out the size of my prison.

The ground was slippery. Soon I stumbled and fell.

Too tired to get up again, I remained there and fell asleep.

*an above-ground grave

Awakening, I felt bread and water beside me. I ate and drank eagerly.
Then I decided to explore further. I would try to cross my prison.

I stepped out care-
fully at first, then
more freely.
Suddenly I stumbled
on the torn hem of
my robe and fell
forward.

I lay on my
face. My
chin rested
on the
prison
floor. But
from my
lips up,
my head
touched
nothing!

I put forward my arm,
and trembled to find
that I had fallen at the
edge of a circular* pit.

A piece of stone fell into the pit. For
seconds I heard it echo far, far below.

*round

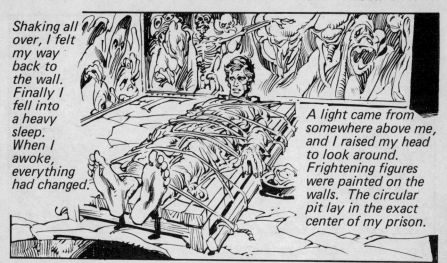

Shaking all over, I felt my way back to the wall. Finally I fell into a heavy sleep. When I awoke, everything had changed.

A light came from somewhere above me, and I raised my head to look around. Frightening figures were painted on the walls. The circular pit lay in the exact center of my prison.

Above me on the high ceiling was painted a figure of old Father Time, with a clock's pendulum* in place of his scythe.**

Was the pendulum, as I first thought, part of the painting? Or did it really move?

A slight noise made me turn my head. Looking at the floor, I saw troops of large rats coming from the pit. They were after some meat that had been left beside me.

*a round piece of metal that swings to and fro in order to regulate a clock
**a long-handled knife-like tool used for cutting grain

When I looked up again, the pendulum was swinging wider—and it had come closer to me!

At its end was a half-circle of steel—like a giant razor blade!

For hours—perhaps days—I watched in terror as it swung above me:

closer . . .

and closer . . .

and yet closer.

And then, almost too late, I began to think. I reached for the remains of the meat and rubbed the straps that were holding me. Then I lay still.

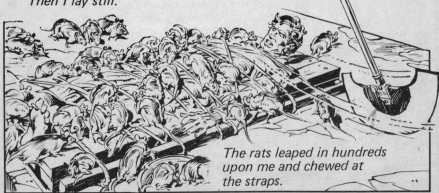

The rats leaped in hundreds upon me and chewed at the straps.

Just as the blade began to cut through my robe, I felt the straps loosen. Carefully I rolled away and off the platform. I was free!

Then the pendulum stopped. It was drawn up to the ceiling. But the metal walls began to glow with heat!

My prison grew terribly hot—and the walls began to close in on me!

I gasped for breath. The burning walls pressed me toward the pit.

Moments later, I trembled on its edge. I was lost. I gave one loud, long, and final scream of terror.

Suddenly there was a loud blast as of many trumpets. With a harsh, grating sound, the walls rushed back. An arm caught mine as I began to fall, fainting, into the pit.

It was the arm of General Lasalle. The French army had entered Toledo.* My enemies had been overthrown, and I was safe at last!

THE END

*a Spanish city where the story-teller had been thrown into prison

The Fall of the House of Usher

The Narrator*

Roderick Usher

Madeline Usher

During the whole of a dark autumn day I had been riding alone through the dreary countryside. I found myself, at evening, near the gloomy old House of Usher. As soon as I saw it, my spirit was struck with sorrow.

*the storyteller

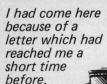

I had come here because of a letter which had reached me a short time before.

Ah! From my old friend Roderick Usher, whom I have not seen for many years!

He suffers from a great illness and a mental problem as well. He wishes my company, as his oldest friend, to cheer him . . .

There is only one answer. I must go to him at once!

So it was that I came to the House of Usher.

A servant took my horse, and I entered the archway of the hall.

Another servant led me in silence through many dark hallways.

On a staircase we met the family doctor. I did not like his look of fear.

Then the servant led me into a large room where his master rose from a couch to greet me.

Roderick!

Ah, my good friend! How delightful to see you!

I gazed at my friend with sorrow at his changed appearance as he told me of his illness.

My senses* are much too sharp. I can eat only the most tasteless food, wear only the softest garments. The smells of flowers are too sweet to bear, and most sounds fill me with horror!

Most of all I fear . . . not danger . . . but the slightest thing which will upset my soul! Sooner or later I will lose life and reason together, fighting fear itself!

But much of his sorrow could be traced to the terrible illness of his beloved sister, who was slowly dying.

She has been my only companion for years. Her death will make me the last of the Ushers!

Her sickness has greatly puzzled the doctors.

She is wasting away to skin and bones . . . she can hardly move . . . she has seizures.**

*taste, touch, sight, hearing, and smell

**sudden attacks of illness which often cause the muscles to cramp

As he spoke, the lady Madeline passed through a far corner of the room without noticing me, and disappeared.

That sight could well have been the last I saw of her, for that night the illness forced her to bed.

For several days I tried to make my friend happy again.

We painted together.

We read together.

Sometimes I listened to him play the guitar.

Then one evening he told me suddenly that the lady Madeline had died.

I want to keep her body for two weeks in one of the vaults* below the house. Later I will bury her in the family graveyard. My friend, will you help me?

Of course, Roderick! Anything!

We carried the body to a vault deep beneath the cellars of the house.

Our torches kept going out because there was so little air in the passageway.

Looking upon her face for the last time, I noted that she seemed almost alive. People with her illness, I knew, often looked like that even after death.

We were twins. Each of us always knew what the other was thinking.

*a storage or burial room

Then we replaced the coffin lid and fastened it tightly.

The great iron door scraped on its hinges as we closed and locked it.

Days of sorrow brought changes in my friend. He roamed from room to room as if he were lost. He stared into space for long hours, as if listening to some sound that was not there.

I felt myself grow frightened at his terror. One night I rose, dressed, and paced the floor, unable to sleep.

It is only this dark room—and the storm outside that keep me from sleeping!

There was a light tap at the door, and Roderick entered. He was very upset.

Come, sit down! I shall read from one of your favorite books, and we will pass away this terrible night together!

In the story, the hero broke into a room: "He so cracked, and ripped, and tore . . . that the noise of the dry wood echoed . . .."

You heard?

It is nothing! The storm!

From below there came a scraping sound . . . and then a hollow clanging.

" . . . a great and terrible ringing sound . . . "

Yet from a distant part of the building, there had come a cracking, ripping noise.

Yes, I hear it! For hours, for days I've heard it—yet I dared not speak!

We have put my sister in her tomb alive!

I heard her first small movements in the coffin, the scraping of the iron hinges, and now her footstep on the stair. *I tell you that she now stands outside the door!*

The heavy doors drew back—
and there stood the figure of
the lady Madeline of Usher,
with blood upon her robes.

With a low, moaning
cry, she fell upon her
brother. Dying for
certain now, she
threw him to the
floor with the weight
of her body. And he,
struck with terror,
died beside her.

I fled from the house,
out across the bridge
and into the storm.

Suddenly behind me there shone a bright light.

It was a blood-red moon, shining through the widening crack in the house.

While I watched, the mighty walls split in two. And finally the pool at my feet closed over the remains of the House of Usher.

THE END

The Cask of Amontillado

Fortunato had harmed me a thousand times. But when he insulted me also, I swore to get even with him. I would kill him—and I would get away with it! Meanwhile, I let him think he was my good friend.

Ah, Fortunato!

Montresor, my dear friend!

One evening during the madness of the carnival season I met him on the street.

Montresor

Fortunato

Above all things, Fortunato considered himself a great judge of old wines. I would get back at him by using a barrel of Amontillado. *

How lucky I met you! I have bought a cask** of what passes for Amontillado, but I have my doubts.

Amontillado? A whole cask? And during the carnival? Impossible!

Amontillado!

I know. I should have spoken to you first. But you were not to be found, and I did not want to miss a great bargain!

I am on my way to Luchesi. He knows wines. He will tell me . . .

Luchesi cannot tell Amontillado from very poor sherry!

Come, let us go to your house. I will check this wine myself!

No, no! I don't want to take up your time.

*a fine sherry wine   **a large barrel

You have a bad cold, and the vaults* are very damp.

The cold is nothing! Amontillado! Let us go!

I allowed him to hurry me to my house.

The place is empty. The servants are all at the carnival.

Taking torches from their holders, we passed down a long, winding staircase into the catacombs** of the Montresors. My friend's steps were unsteady from drink.

Steady, my friend! Don't slip.

The Amontillado! I can hardly believe it!

Soon a coughing spell forced Fortunato to stop.

Come, we must go back! The cold is bad for your cough.

Cough! Cough!

Your health is important! You are rich, respected, admired. You will be ill . . .

The cough is nothing! I shall not die of a cough!

*underground rooms used for storing wine and other things
**underground rooms used for burying the bodies of family members

Taking a bottle of wine from a rack nearby, I knocked off the neck and offered it to Fortunato. He drank eagerly.

True! And a drink of this wine will protect us from the damp!

Three sides were lined with bodies. From the fourth, the bones had been thrown down and lay upon the earth.

He took my arm and we walked on, passing through low arches. At last we reached a deep cave with air so bad that our torches would hardly burn.

Go ahead! The Amontillado is in there!

He stepped forward, but stopped at the rock wall. In it were two iron hooks, a chain, and a padlock. In a second I had wrapped the chain around his waist and fastened him there.

Pass your hand over the wall. It is *very* damp. If you don't want to go back, then I must leave you!

The Amontillado!

Digging into the pile of bones, I took out building stones, cement, and a trowel.* Then I began to wall up the entrance to the cave.

There was a low, moaning cry from inside and a great rattling of chains. I sat down and waited.

Ahhhhhhhh! Montresor! Montresor!

At last the clanking stopped. I continued my work. Finally there was only one stone to be fitted in. There came from the cave a low laugh and a sad voice.

Ha! Ha! Ha! A very good joke indeed! We will have many a laugh about it at the carnival, over our wine . . .

The Amontillado?

*a tool for spreading cement on brick or stone

Ha! Ha! Yes, the Amontillado. But is it not getting late? Will they not be waiting for us, Lady Fortunato and the rest? Let us be gone.

Yes, let us be gone.

FOR THE LOVE OF HEAVEN, MONTRESOR!

Yes, Fortunato.

There was no answer. I forced the last stone into its place. I plastered it up. Against the new wall I piled the old bones.

For half a century, no one has disturbed them.

The End

The Murders in the Rue Morgue

This was the scene * of the murders in which the Paris police found themselves without a clue. My friend Dupin would solve the case by using his reason alone.

The Narrator

Dupin

French Sailor

*place where something happens

Living in Paris in the spring of 1800, I visited a book shop one day in search of a special title.

Ah, monsieur* . . . it is very rare and hard to find. I regret I do not have it!

This gentleman has just asked for the same book!

C. Auguste Dupin, monsieur, at your service.

I am happy to meet you, sir. Perhaps we should get together for our search.

So it was that Dupin and I became friends.

*mister

*We found many interests in common. At last we moved into an apartment together in an old house on the Faubourg St. Germain. * It was here that we first read of the murders in the Rue Morgue. **

You read about the strange affair in the Rue Morgue?

A murder, wasn't it?

Murder, yes, but not of the usual kind.

Come! Picture this, if you will! About three o'clock this morning, the neighbors were awakened by terrible cries from the fourth floor of a house in the Rue Morgue . . .

Awful sounds, they were . . . like someone being killed!

Who lives there?

Madame L'Espanaye and her daughter Camille!

*a French street name

When no one answered the bell, the door was broken open.

Easy! That does it!

The cries had stopped. But as the men rushed up the first flight of stairs, they heard a new sound.

Listen!

It sounds like two men arguing!

But the sounds stopped, and all was quiet. The men ran through the house, searching from room to room. At last they came to a large back room on the fourth floor.

Locked— from the inside!

We must break it down.

The room was a terrible mess. The furniture was broken and thrown about.

What has happened?

There is no one here!

But where are the ladies?

A bloody razor!

Locks of hair—gray, human hair—covered with blood!

A policeman picked up two bags from the floor.

Gold! At least four thousand francs* in gold!

A safe—but open!

Nothing here but a few old letters.

But Madame L'Espanaye and her daughter! Where are they?

A great deal of soot seems to have been knocked down in the fire-place . . .

Do you think . . . oh, no!

*French money

Yes . . . it is here. A body!

The body was dragged out and examined.

She is cut and scratched, no doubt from the chimney. But it seems she has been choked to death.

The body of the daughter had been forced up the narrow chimney opening. It was still quite warm.

After searching the rest of the house without finding anything else, the group made its way into a small paved yard in the rear.

It is the old lady— Madame L'Espanaye!

But who could know her now!

Madame had been badly beaten. Her throat had been so deeply cut that her head was almost separated from her body.

To this terrible murder there is not yet the smallest clue.

We looked eagerly for the next day's newspapers. Though nothing had been found, an account was given of the people who had been questioned.

There was Pauline Dubourg, a washer-woman.

Yes, I am Pauline Dubourg. I have washed clothes for the L'Espanayes for three years.

I used to pick up the clothes and bring them to my home to wash.

How did the mother and daughter get along together?

Why, very well! They always seemed very kind to each other.

Did you ever see any other person in the house?

Never at all! There was no servant, and I never saw a visitor.

Were they well off? Did they have money?

They paid me well, that is all I know! As for what people say, Madame was thought to have some money saved up. I believe she told fortunes for a living.

Very well. We will write out what you have said. Please come to the station to sign it.

Goodbye, monsieur.

Also questioned was Pierre Moreau, a seller of tobacco.

All my life I have lived in the area, yes. Madame L'Espanaye has bought small amounts of tobacco from me for perhaps four years.

Madame owned the house, and they say she had money.

They also say the old lady told fortunes. But I don't believe it.

And why not?

Yes, I see.

They lived a very quiet life. I have hardly seen anyone enter the door but the old lady and her daughter. A person came once or twice to deliver packages, and eight or ten times a doctor came.

It seems that many other neighbors said the same thing: that no one ever came to the house.

The shutters of the front windows were seldom open. Those in the rear were always closed, except for the one large back room on the fourth floor.

Isadore Muset, the policeman who first entered the house, made his report.

After breaking into the house, I led the way upstairs. Upon reaching the first landing, I heard two voices, loud and angry . . .

One was gruff,* the other high and thin—a very strange voice!

The first voice was that of a Frenchman. The second was that of a foreigner**—man or woman, I could not tell. I believe the language was Spanish.

Henri Duval, a neighbor who entered the house, agreed with Muset except about the voices.

The higher voice, man or woman I don't know. But I think the person spoke Italian.

It was not Madame L'Espanaye or her daughter?

No, no! It was not French, and it was not the L'Espanayes! I have spoken with them many times!

*low and harsh
**someone from another country

A Dutchman* passing by had joined the search of the house. Not speaking French, he was questioned in Dutch.

Monsieur Odenheimer agrees with the other reports except about the voices. He says the high voice was that of a man—a Frenchman!

William Bird, an Englishman who had lived for two years in Paris, had also passed by and joined the search. He was one of the first up the stairs.

The higher voice was very loud. It was certainly not that of an Englishman. It seemed to me to be German, but man or woman, I could not tell.

Monsieur Bird speaks German?

No, not at all.

*someone from Holland

Also questioned was Alfonzo Garcio, a Spanish undertaker* who lived in the Rue Morgue.

You speak English, sir?

No, no! I judge by the kind of sound.

I entered the house but I did not go up the stairs. I am too nervous! You understand?

But you could hear the voices?

Oh, yes, very well! The high voice was that of an Englishman. Of this I am sure!

Alberto Montani, a seller of candy, was also one of the first to go up the stairs.

The high voice? It was quick and uneven. I think it was the voice of a Russian.

Do you know Russian?

*someone who prepares bodies to be buried

No, monsieur. I am an Italian. I have never spoken with a native of Russia!

Jules Mignaud, a banker of the firm of Mignaud et Fils, also spoke to the police.

About Madame L'Espanaye, monsieur . . .

Madame L'Espanaye opened an account eight years ago. She owned some property.

She took nothing out until three days before her death, when she came for the sum of 4,000 francs.

This sum was paid in gold, and a clerk took her home with the money.

May I talk with the clerk?

Certainly! Send in Le Bon!

Yes, I am Adolphe Le Bon. I went with Madame L'Espanaye and carried the two bags of gold to her home.

Did you enter the house?

No, monsieur. Her daughter met us at the door and took one of the bags, while the old lady took the other. I then bowed and left.

Now think carefully. Was there anyone else in sight—anyone going by?

There was no one at all! It is a side street, and very lonely.

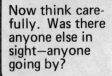

Paul Dumas, a doctor, also made a report.

I was called in about dawn to view the bodies. That of the young lady was much cut and scraped. That it had been forced up the chimney would account for it.

There were deep scratches below the chin, with a series of spots which must have been the marks of fingers.

I think that Mademoiselle L'Espanaye was strangled to death.

The body of the mother was terribly cut up. The bones on the right side were nearly all broken. The whole body was discolored.

A heavy club, a bar of iron, a chair: such a weapon in the hands of a strong man might have given such results. No woman could have done it.

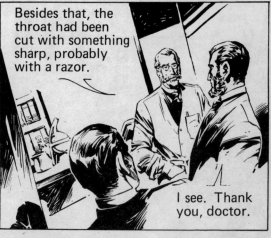

Besides that, the throat had been cut with something sharp, probably with a razor.

I see. Thank you, doctor.

The paper says that a murder so strange has never before been committed in Paris! There is not the shadow of a clue . . .

So who can solve it?

Later, the evening paper brought the news that although there were no new clues, Adolphe Le Bon had been arrested.

Let us check into these murders ourselves! Le Bon helped me once, for which I am grateful.

We will go and see the house with our own eyes. I know the chief of police, and shall have no trouble being allowed to do so.

Very well.

We reached the Rue Morgue in the late afternoon. There were still many people looking up at the house.

We walked through an alley and came to the rear of the house. Dupin looked around with great interest.

Ah!

Returning to the front door, we were let in by the police. We went up to the bedroom where the bodies still lay. Dupin looked at everything, including the bodies.

H'm . . .

On the way home we stopped at the offices of Le Monde, *a daily paper read by sailors and ship's captains.*

Wait for me. I'll be only a moment.

LE MONDE

Upon reaching home, Dupin would not talk about the murders until noon the next day. Then he made a surprising remark.

The police find this case hard to solve because it is so strange. But that very thing will lead me—or has already led me—to solve it!

I am waiting for a person who must have known about these crimes. I look for the man here—in this room—any moment now.

If he comes, we must keep him here. Here are some guns. We both know how to use them.

Scarcely believing what I heard, I took the gun, and Dupin continued.

There was the report of the two voices heard in argument. What was the strangest part of that report?

Everyone agreed that one man was a Frenchman. But everyone disagreed on the second, or higher voice.

Not only did they disagree, but each of these men, from five different countries, thought the voice spoke a foreign language!

Not a single word could be understood! This gives us a great clue!

Then—the room. The doors were locked from inside; there were no secret exits. The chimneys were too narrow to let a cat through. The killers *must* have left through the windows!

But the police found them nailed shut—from the inside!

They found that they could not force the windows up. There was a large nail through the window frame and sill of each one.

Well?

But I removed the nail, and I still could not force the window up! I looked for, and found, a hidden spring keeping it shut.

In the case of the window behind the bed, some years ago, the nail had been broken in two. Although it remained in place and looked whole, it no longer held the window shut.

If someone got away through that window, and let it close behind him, the hidden spring would lock the window. Yet it would seem that the nail was doing so!

So you have solved that part of it! But how did the killer get down?

A killer who was a good climber could have used the outside shutter to swing himself from the window to the lightning rod. It runs from the roof to the ground nearby. He could have climbed down the rod!

So we have a killer with a strange voice who is a good climber. He also has great strength and is stupid enough to leave four thousand francs in gold behind him!

He is a madman! Someone who has escaped from a mental hospital!

Look at this lock of hair which I removed from Madame L'Espanaye's fingers!

I removed the hair from the envelope and looked at it carefully.

Dupin! This is not human hair!

I did not say it was. Now read from this book.

It described the large orang-outang ape of the East Indian islands. The animal had great size, strength, and agility.* I understood the full story of the murders at last.

Yes, I see. But what of the second voice, the Frenchman?

I suppose him to be a sailor, the owner of the animal. He must know something of the murders.

Perhaps it got away from him and he followed it. It is probably still loose. I left this advertisement at the newspaper last night. I think it will bring him here.

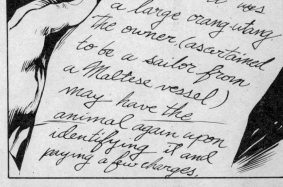

it was a large orang-utang. the owner, (ascertained to be a sailor from a Maltese vessel) may have the animal again upon identifying it and paying a few charges.

At this moment we heard a step upon the stairs.

Be ready with your gun, but do not show or use it unless I tell you to.

*ability to move and climb easily

Good evening.

Come in! Sit down! I suppose you've come about the orang-outang?

A fine animal— I envy you! How old is he?

I have no way of telling—four or five years, per- haps. You have him here?

Oh, no. He is at a stable nearby.

I don't want you to go through this for nothing. I'm very willing to pay a reward.

My reward shall be this. You shall tell me all you know about the murders in the Rue Morgue!

My friend, we mean you no harm. I know you did not kill those women. But an innocent* man is now in jail. He is charged with a crime of which you can point out the killer!

So help me, I will tell you all I know. I *am* innocent of this crime!

He told us that he had brought the animal home from a recent voyage. He had kept it safely at his Paris home until it recovered from a foot wound. Then he planned to sell it. It was kept in a cage in an open closet.

But coming home late one night, he found the animal in his bedroom. It was imitating its master shaving!

Terrified at seeing the animal holding a razor, the sailor brought out a whip he sometimes used to control it.

*someone who has done nothing wrong

But seeing the whip, the animal sprang through the door of the room, ran down the stairs, and jumped through an open window into the street.

Still carrying the razor, the ape led the sailor on a chase through the empty city streets. At last, seeing a lighted window, it rushed into a back yard in the Rue Morgue.

Catching sight of a lightning rod, it climbed up.

Reaching the fourth floor, it grasped a shutter and swung itself over and through the window.

The sailor climbed the rod easily, but as he did so, terrible screams came from the room. He could not reach the window, but could only look in.

Angered by her screams, the ape swept the razor across the old lady's throat.

Then, its anger made worse by the sight of blood, the ape grabbed the daughter, who had fainted, and choked her.

At this point, hearing the shouts of its owner, and looking up to see his face through the window, the ape's anger turned to fear. It rushed around the room knocking things over and breaking the furniture.

As if to hide what it had done, it thrust the body of the daughter up the chimney. Then it threw the old lady's body out the window.

The sailor quickly slid down the rod.

Terrified at what he had seen, he ran home, leaving the orang-outang to its fate. The ape must have left the room just before the door was broken in.

The next day we heard that the orang-outang had been caught. Its owner then sold it for a good sum.

When we told our story to the chief of police, Le Bon was let go at once.

You are free to go, Monsieur Le Bon.

A thousand thanks, Monsieur Dupin!

It was nothing at all.

The chief made a few remarks about the need for people to mind their own business, but Dupin said nothing.

Let him talk. It will make him feel better. I am happy that I solved the case before he could do so!

The END

words to know

tomb	scythe	cask	scene
circular	seizures	catacombs	francs
pendulum	vaults	trowel	gruff
foreigner	undertaker	agility	innocent

questions

1. In *"The Pit and the Pendulum,"* we are not told why the central character has been thrown into prison. But can you tell anything about those who put him there from the punishments he had to suffer?

2. In *"The Fall of the House of Usher,"* why was the story-teller called to his friend's home? What did he learn about the brother and sister when he arrived?

3. When Madeline seemed to have died, what two things made Roderick Usher fear that his sister might still be alive?

4. Why do you think the house collapsed once Roderick and Madeline died?

5. In *"The Cask of Amontillado,"* how did Montresor first get Fortunato down into the vaults below his house? How did Montresor keep him going even though Fortunato was coughing and it was difficult to breathe?

6. Why did Montresor want to kill Fortunato? How did he finally do it? Do you think he was ever caught?

7. What was the single biggest clue that Dupin in *"The Murders in the Rue Morgue"* used to figure out the killer's identity?

8. What was the purpose of placing an advertisement in a seaman's newspaper?